Sally Kindberg's

DRAW IT! PIRATES

BLOOMSBURY
Activity Books

To young sea dogs everywhere

AVAST THERE!

Draw shipwrecks, sharks and bad behaviour. Jump on board and join the ghastly crew!

Burbling bilgewater! Fear for your lives when you cross paths – and swords – with loathsome lady pirates.

Meet mermaids and monsters,
look for treasure and do try
not to walk the plank.

Draw some crew on this pirate ship.

Draw who you'd like to be your First Mate.

Pirates believed having a swallow tattoo meant you'd reach land safely after a voyage.

Draw a pet for a pirate.

How many more pirate ships can you fit on these pages?

YUM! Seaweed sandwiches, barnacle burgers and octopus stew are on the pirates' lunch menu today. Draw them!

Draw some gruesome pirate punishments.

Giant squid have big bulgy eyeballs and beaks as sharp as knives … Ouch! A preserved squid called Archie, more than 8m long, can be seen in London's Natural History Museum.

Draw a map of where the treasure's hidden.

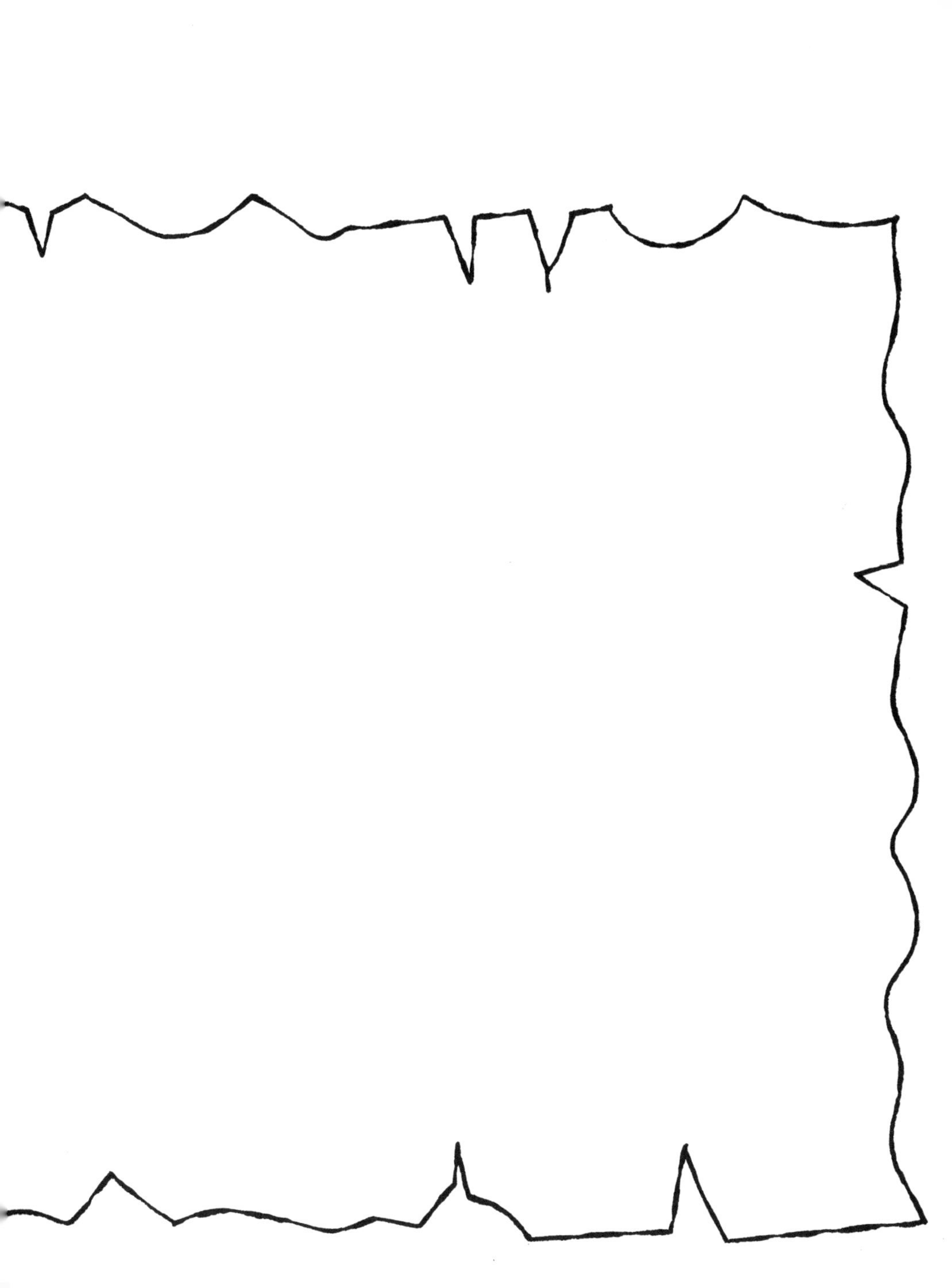

Draw the Jolly Roger (skull and crossbones) on this flag.

Draw some
weapons for this
ghastly pirate crew.
Scurvy
dog!

Draw a shark looking for lunch.

Draw someone walking the plank.

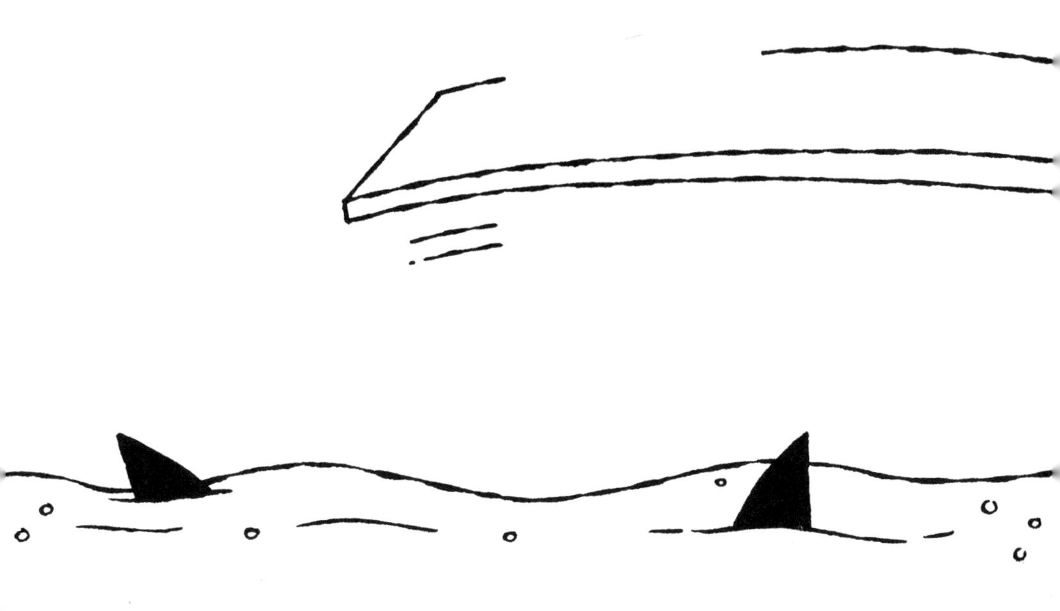

Anne Bonney and
Mary Read disguised
themselves as boys
and became fearsome
pirates. Draw them
in this ship's rigging!
Draw us . . .
or else!

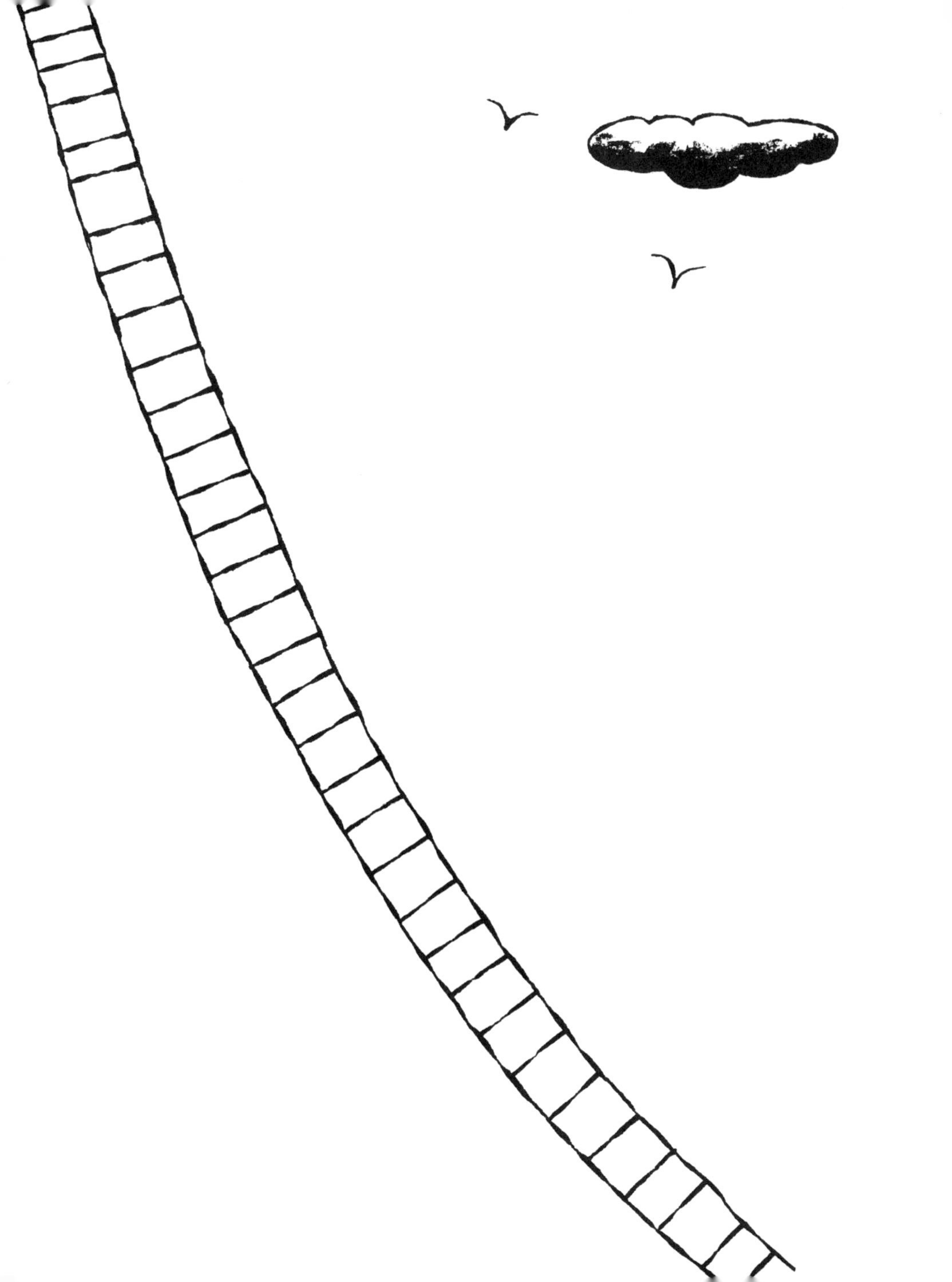

Henry Morgan was known as Blackbeard the pirate and terrified his enemies with his fearsome beard. Draw him!

at night . . .

Who's in this hammock?

Draw what you'd do if you were
marooned by pirates on an island.

WHOOPS! Someone's fallen overboard, and the sea is full of . . . what?

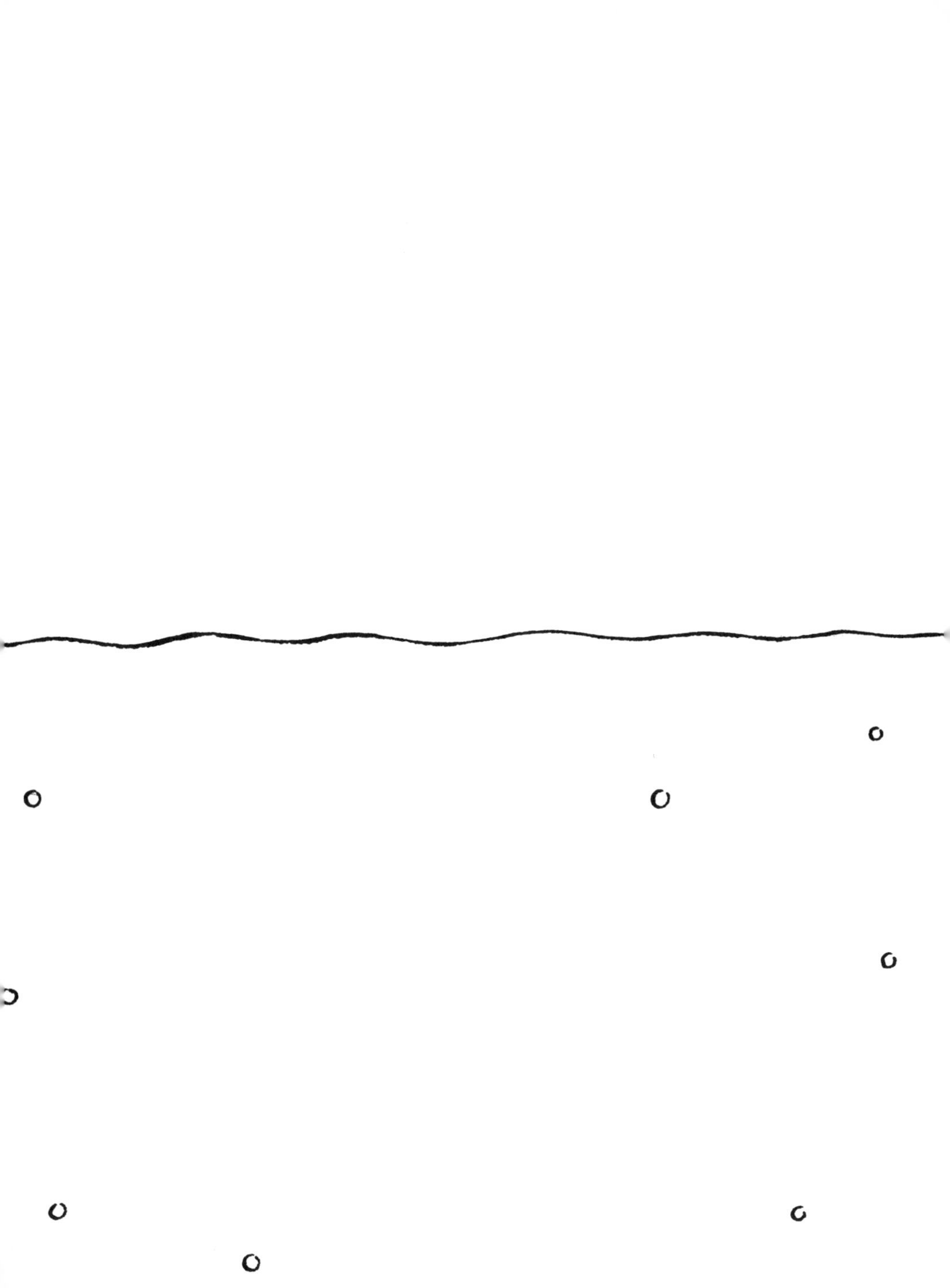

Draw some juggling pirates.
Phew!

This pirate's having a bad hair day. Draw what she'd look like after a makeover.

Draw a shipwreck under the sea.

Draw some pirates dancing.

Draw what or who you'd
rescue if your ship was sinking.

It's said pirates liked to drink a mixture of gunpowder and rum. Yuk!

Draw a label for this bottle of it.

Draw a pirate
with a headache.

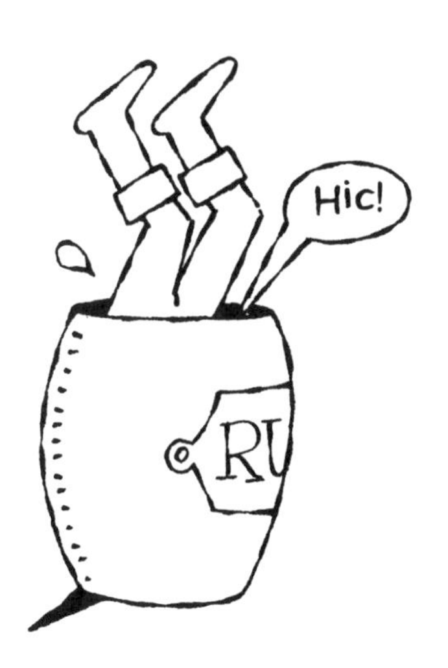

Draw the pirate ship Nasty Nigel.

Draw an unusual pirate being kind.

Draw Davey Jones' locker
(the bottom of the sea)

Draw some toys for this baby pirate.

Draw a pirate
on a bike – his
ship's just sailed
without him!

Draw what's in these treasure chests.

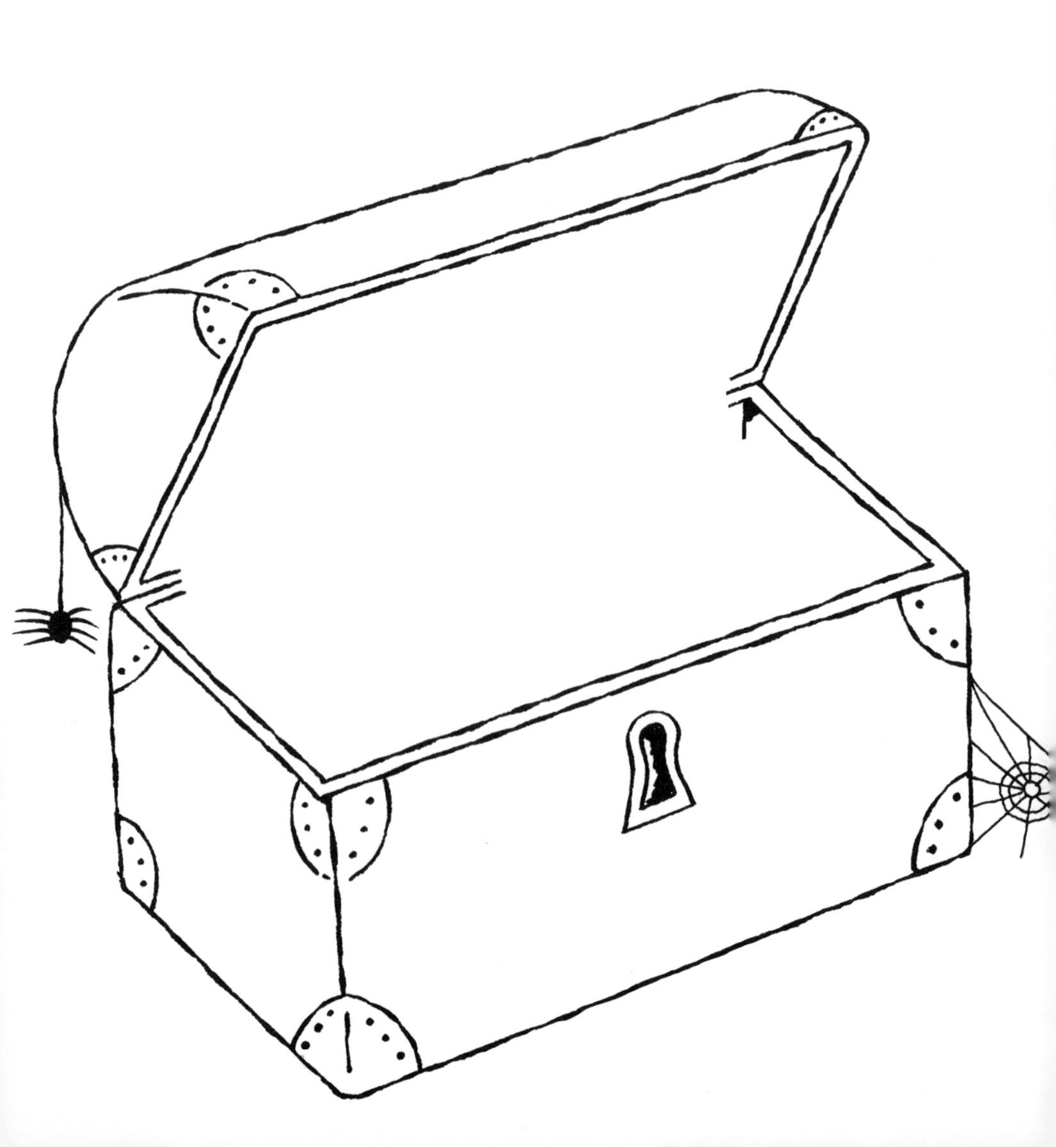

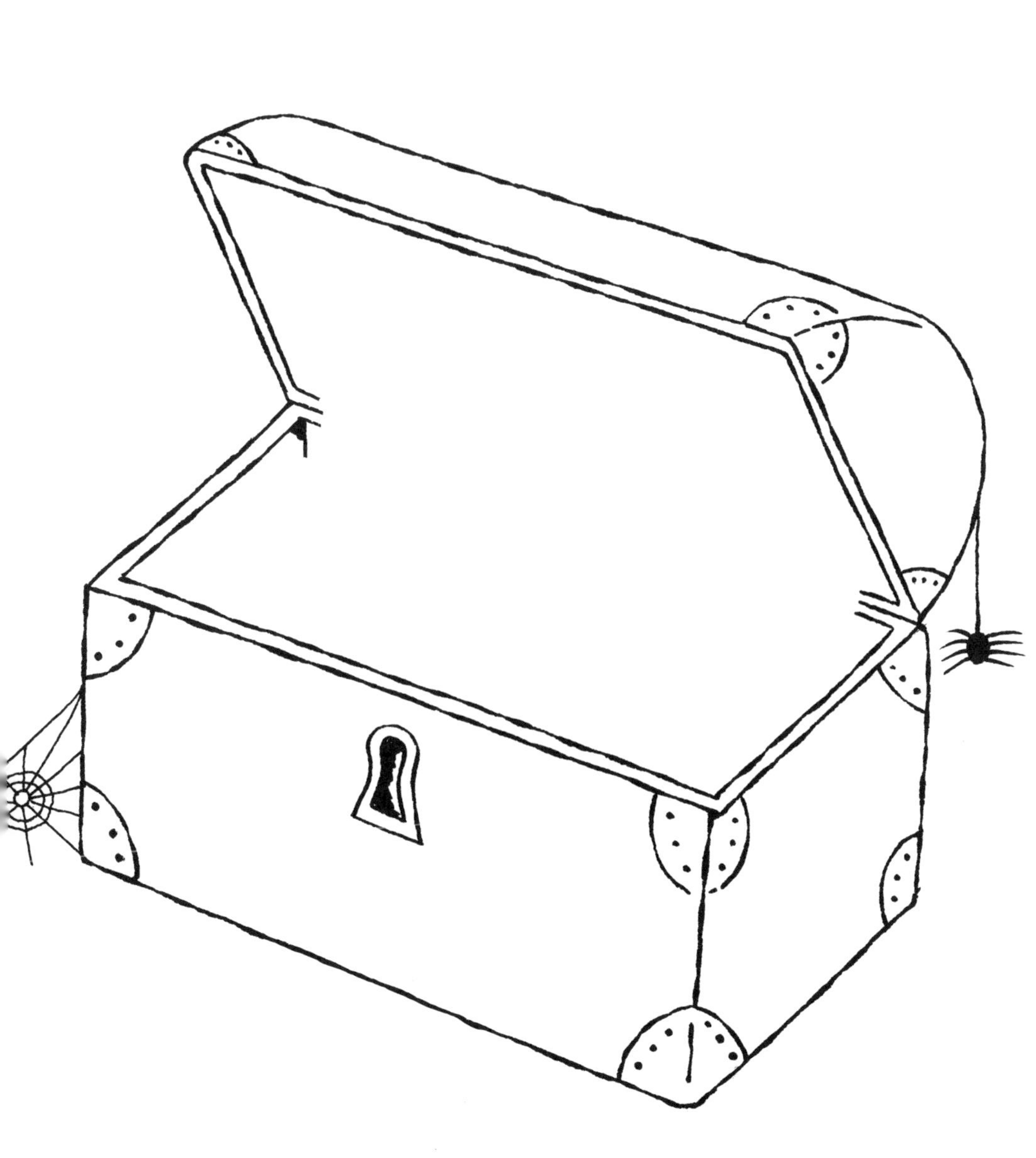

Draw four must-have items for a young pirate.

Pirate 'Black Sam' Bellamy's gold treasure was discovered in Cape Cod three hundred years after his ship sank.

Draw what these pirates caught on their fishing lines.

You've been ship-wrecked but you've managed to make a raft. Draw it!

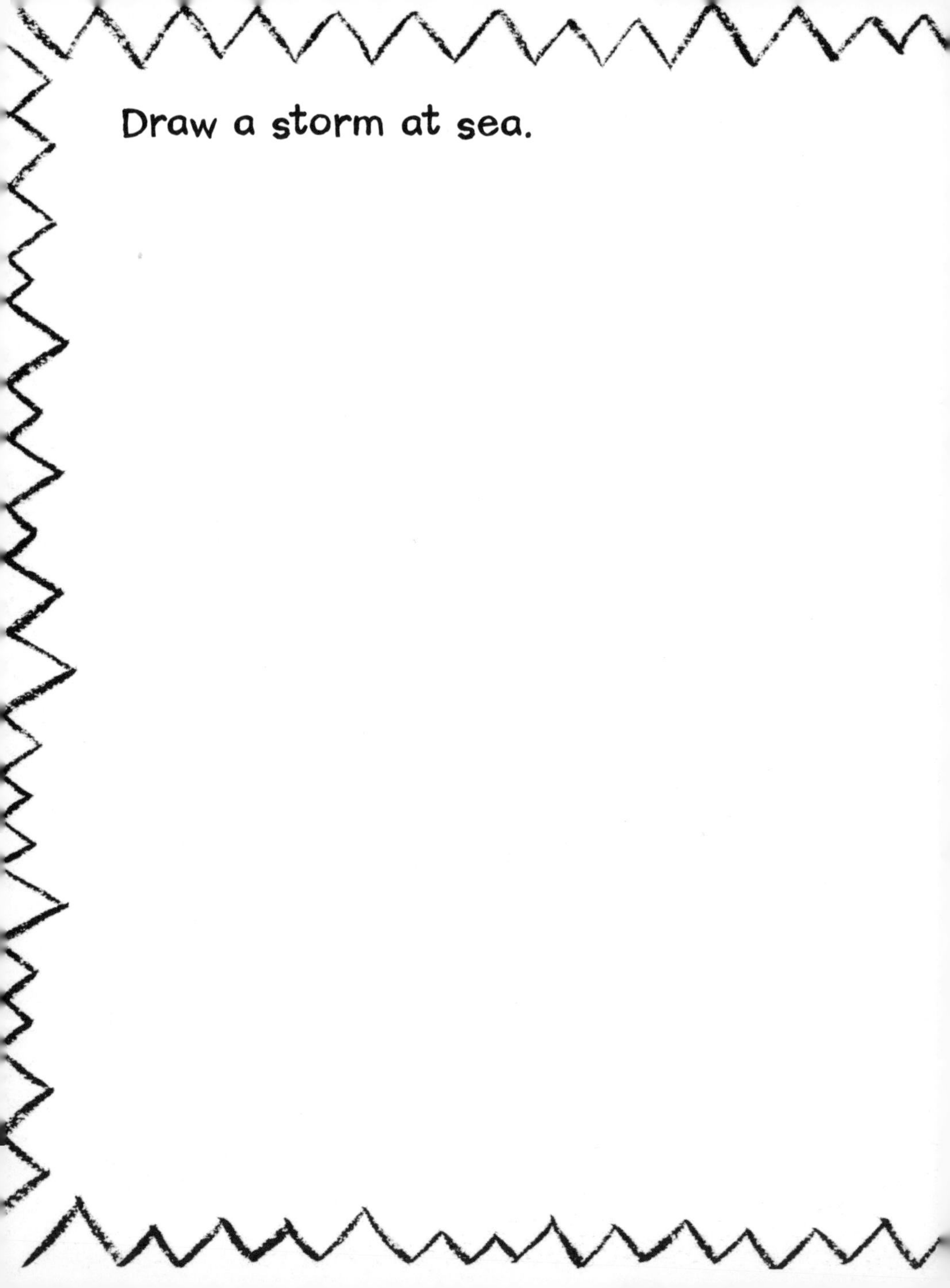
Draw a storm at sea.

Draw a sea
monster.

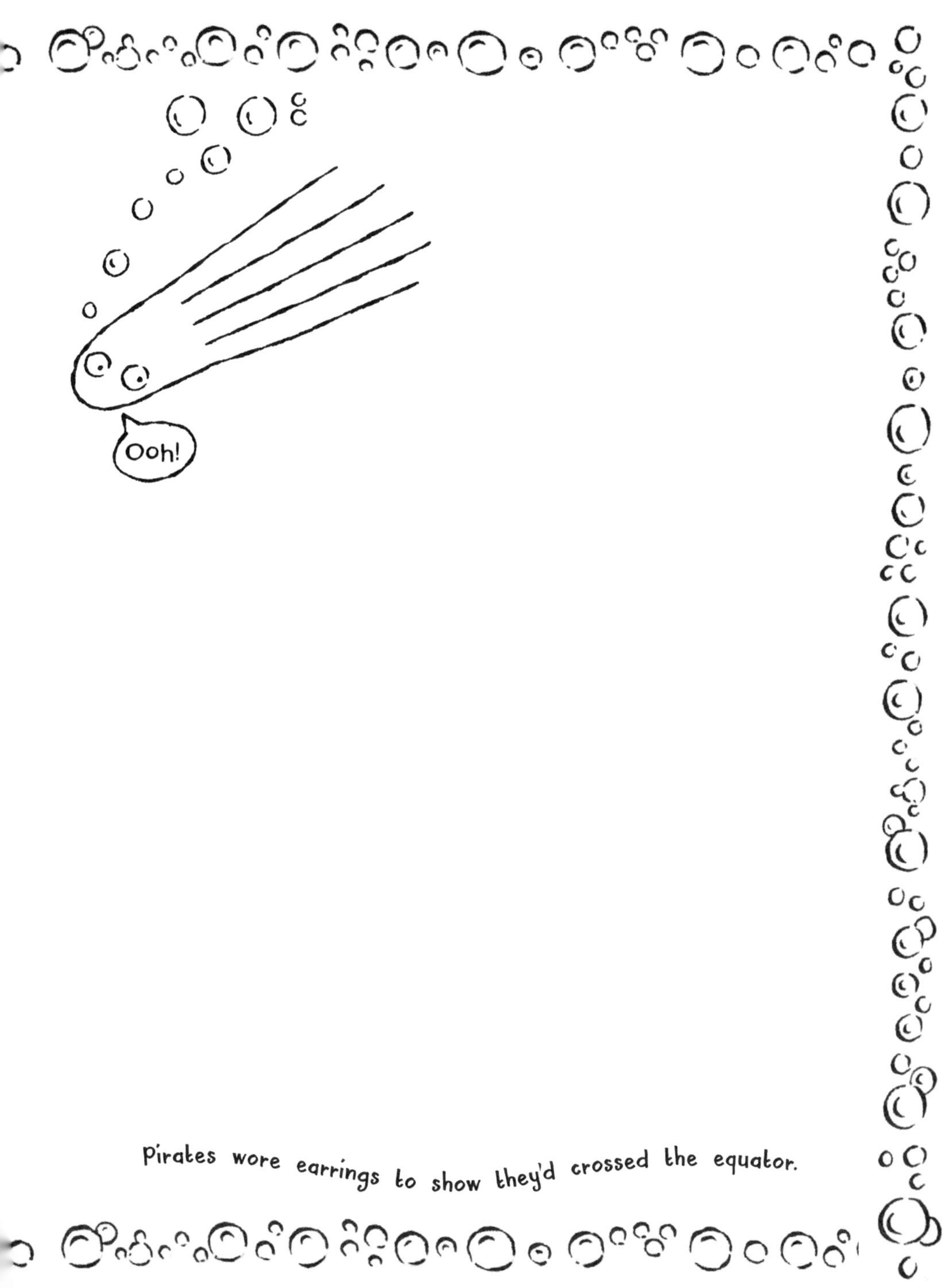
Ooh!
Pirates wore earrings to show they'd crossed the equator.

Draw some pirates having a tug o'war competition — no cheating, Big Arthur!

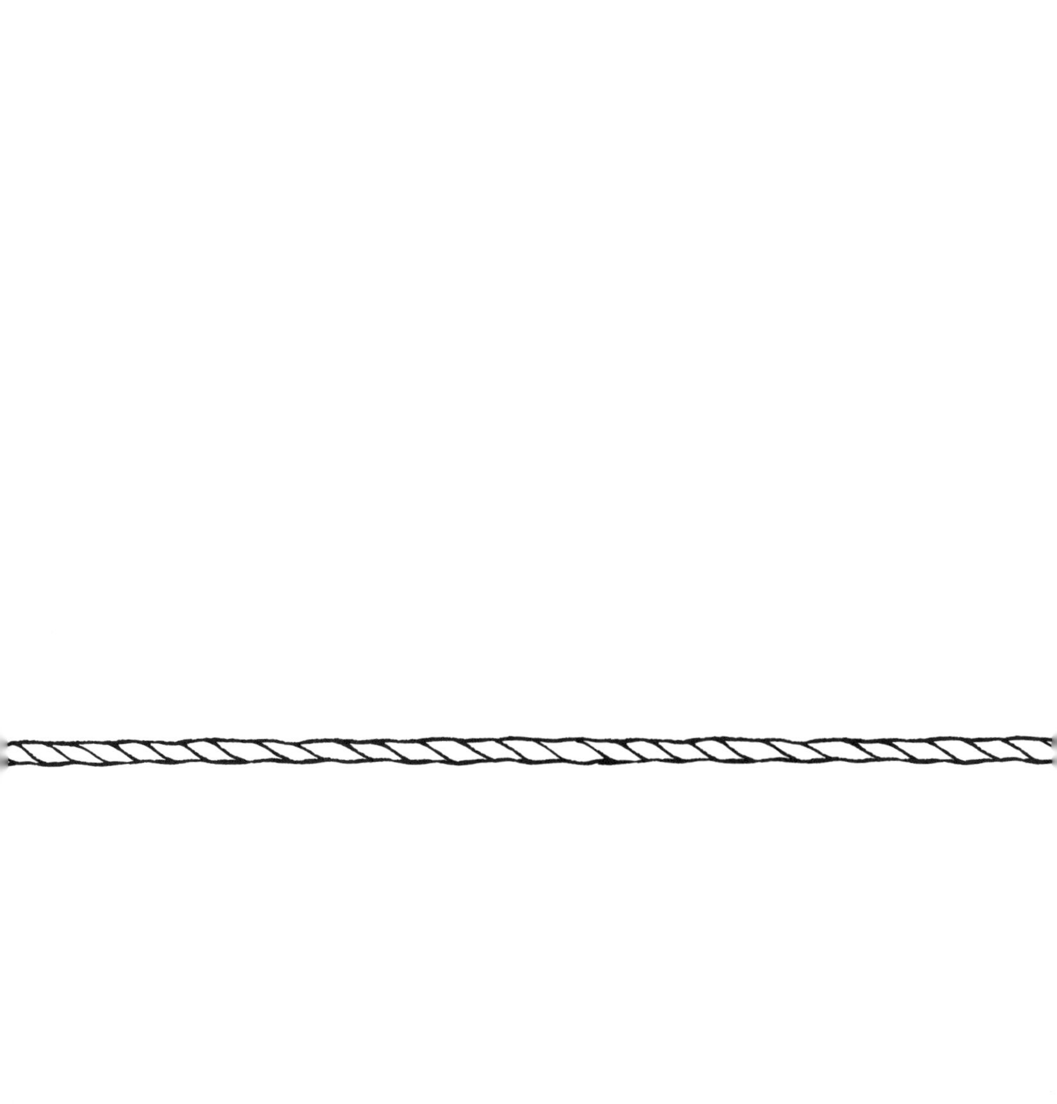

WHOOPS!

Someone's lost
their peg-leg.
Draw its owner.

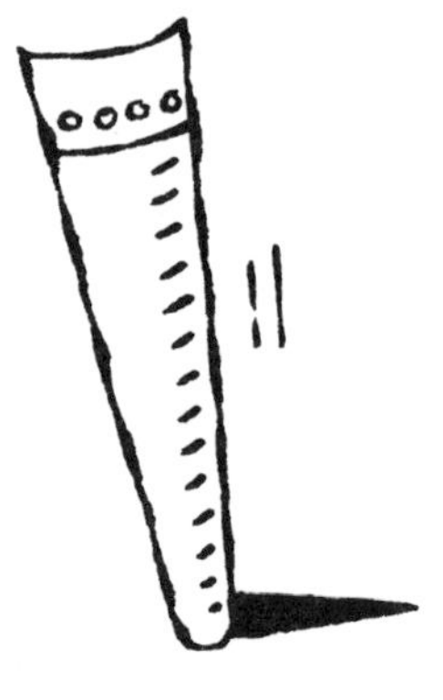

Draw what the pirate captain's parrot is saying.

Draw a pirate's dream.

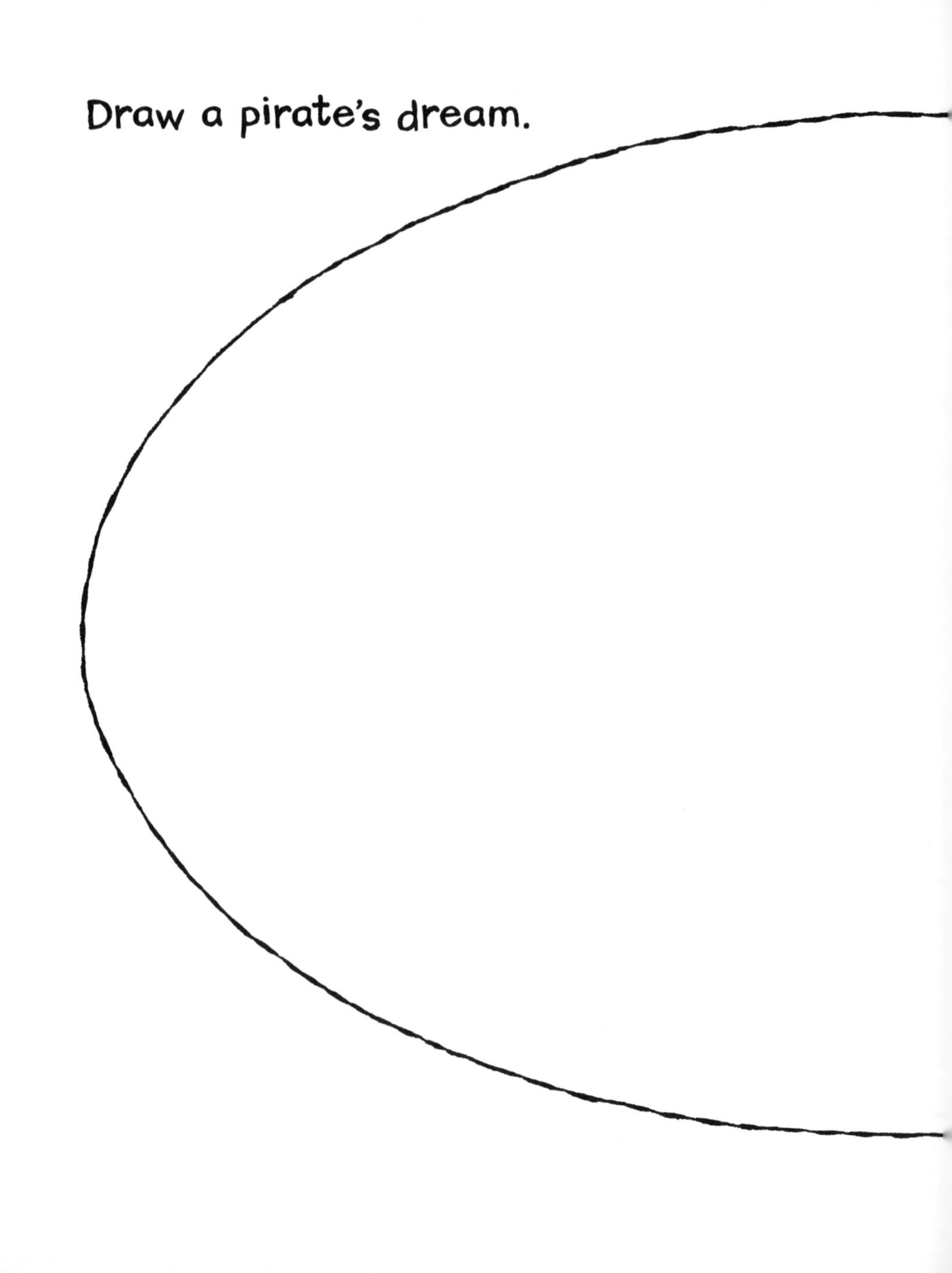

Zzzzzz
Pooh!

A cabin boy always has to do the worst jobs on board. Draw a couple of them.

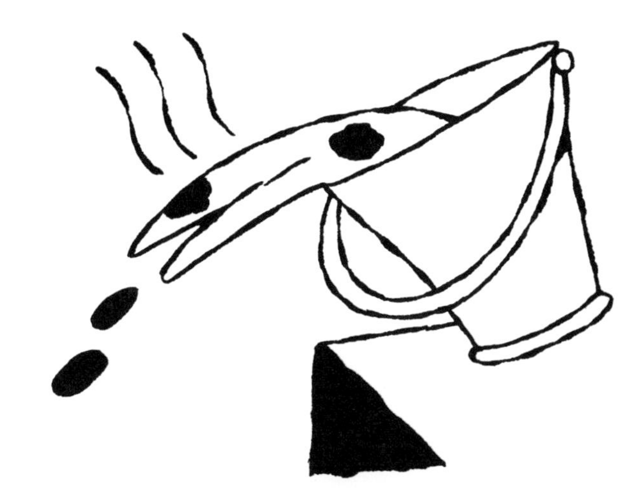

Draw who's saying what.

AVAST THERE YE BILGE RAT!

GET BELOW DECKS YE LUBBER!

AHOY MATEY!

ARRR!

ARRR!

Pirates have disguised their ship so they can creep into the harbour. Draw it!

Draw some pirates doing press-ups.

Draw what a pirate fears the most.

I DON'T LIKE BEING TICKLED ACTUALLY
Gah!

The pirates have seen some mermaids – or so they say! Draw them

All that bad behaviour can be very stressful. Draw a pirate doing yoga.

Draw an anchor for this ship.

No whistling on board ship!
It was thought to bring bad luck and stormy weather.

Draw some fancy tattoos on this pirate's arms.
I hope it doesn't hurt

Draw this mermaid's song.

Draw a pirate's
party trick.

Draw a ship's figurehead and some seagulls hitching a ride on this pirate ship.

Good Grief! Who else is taking part in the tug o' war competition?

AHOY MATEY!
GET BELOW DECKS YE LUBBER!

GET BELOW DECKS YE LUBBER!
SHIVER ME TIMBERS!
ARRR!
SEASICK PILLS
AHOY MATEY!
AVAST THERE YE BILGE RAT!

MUM
Hic!

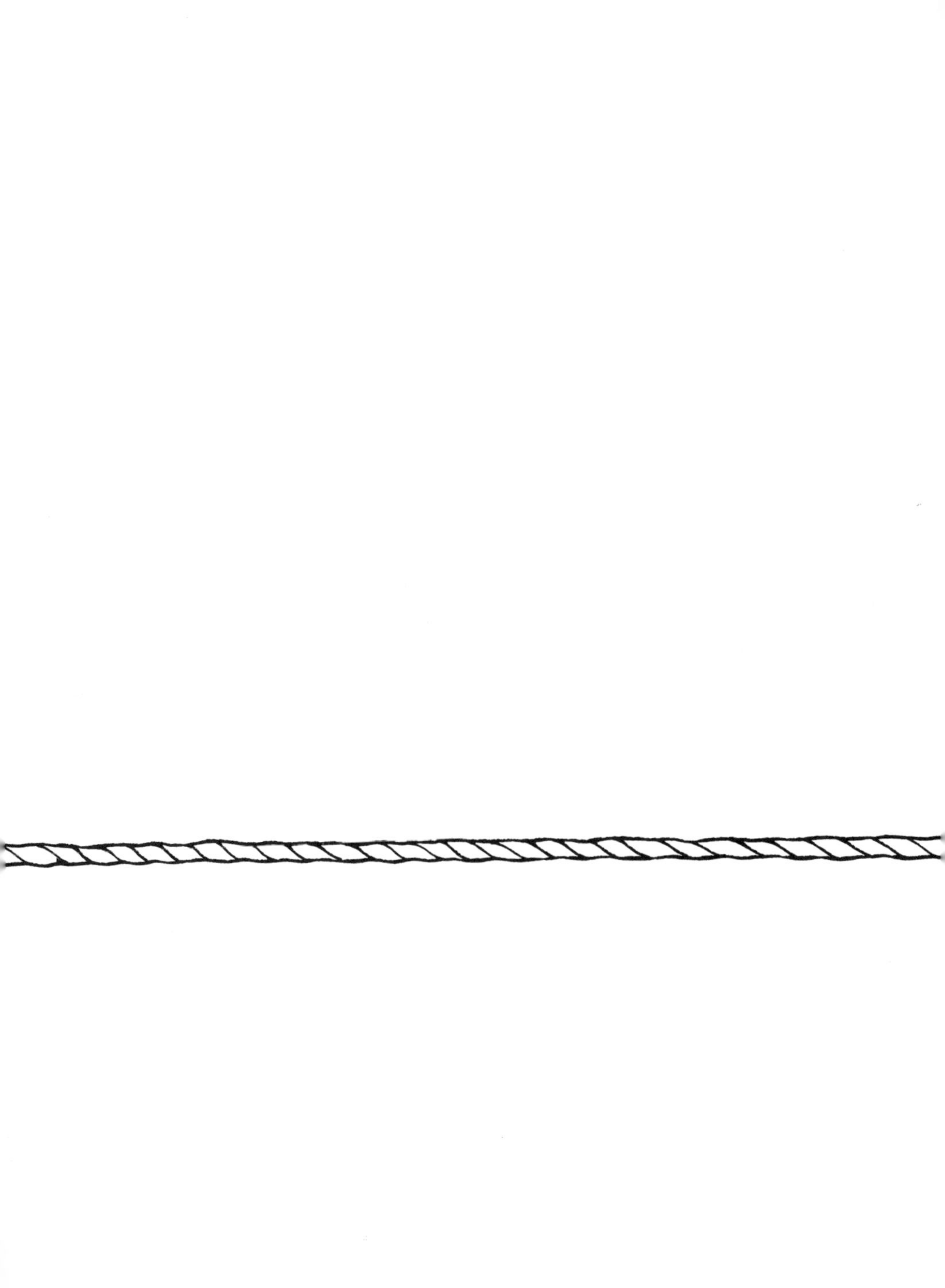

There's no wind blowing and you can't sail anywhere, so the bored pirates are counting dolphins.

How many dolphins can you fit onto these pages?

The sea's very rough and some pirates are feeling seasick. URGH!! Draw them.

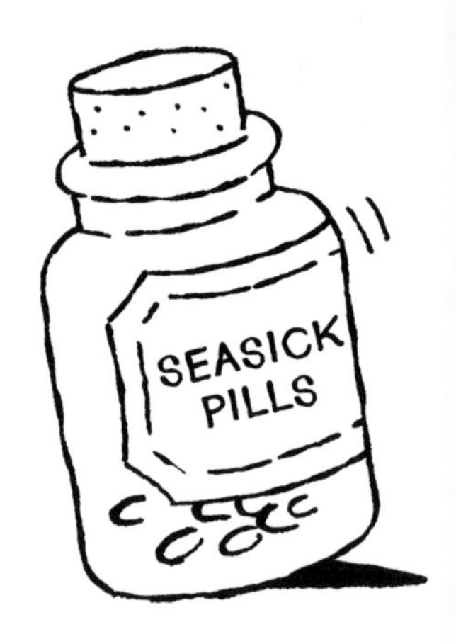

Draw a pirate's joke.

Draw a pirate roller-skating on deck.

Draw who's in the Crow's Nest.

This pirate looked through his telescope and saw . . . what?

The Caribbean Island of Roatan was a pirate headquarters, where 5000 pirates were said to live at one time.

AARGH!
Giant squid attack!
Draw it!

Draw a flag for your very own pirate ship.

Draw a pirate's pyjamas.

Draw some pirates in space.

Draw some specs for this short-sighted pirate.

Draw a pirate with toothache (if he's got any teeth that is).

Draw what else you saw when
you were looking for treasure.

The waters around these islands are full of . . . what?

Make up some names for these pirates.

Draw what happened next in this pirate's comic.

Draw Capt'n Fearsome Norman's first swimming lesson.

Pirate brothers Scurvy Charlie, One-Eyed Billy and Stinky Squealer want to buy a birthday present for their mother. Draw what they chose.

Draw some maggots in this sandwich.

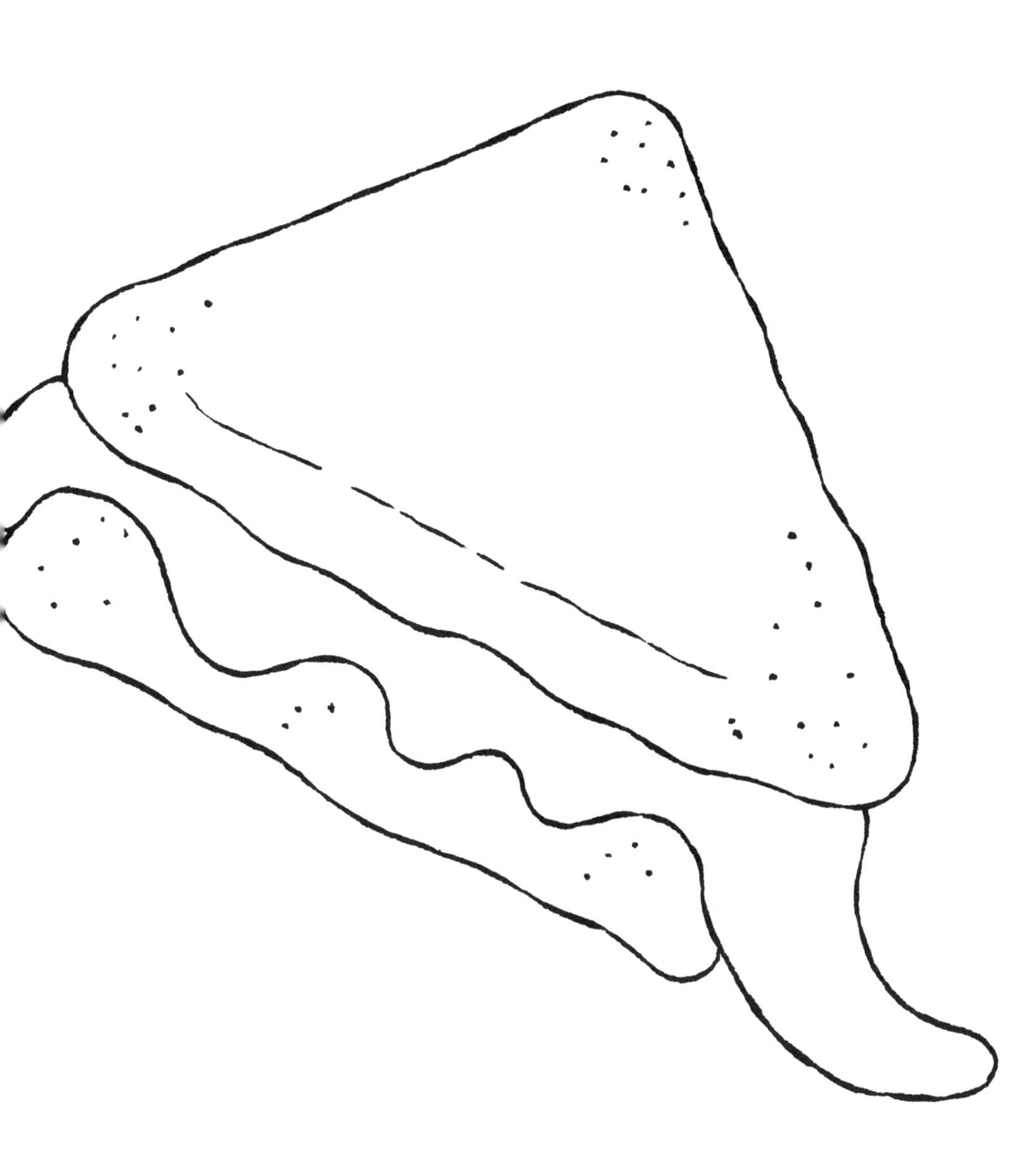

Draw some patterns on
these pirates' scarves.

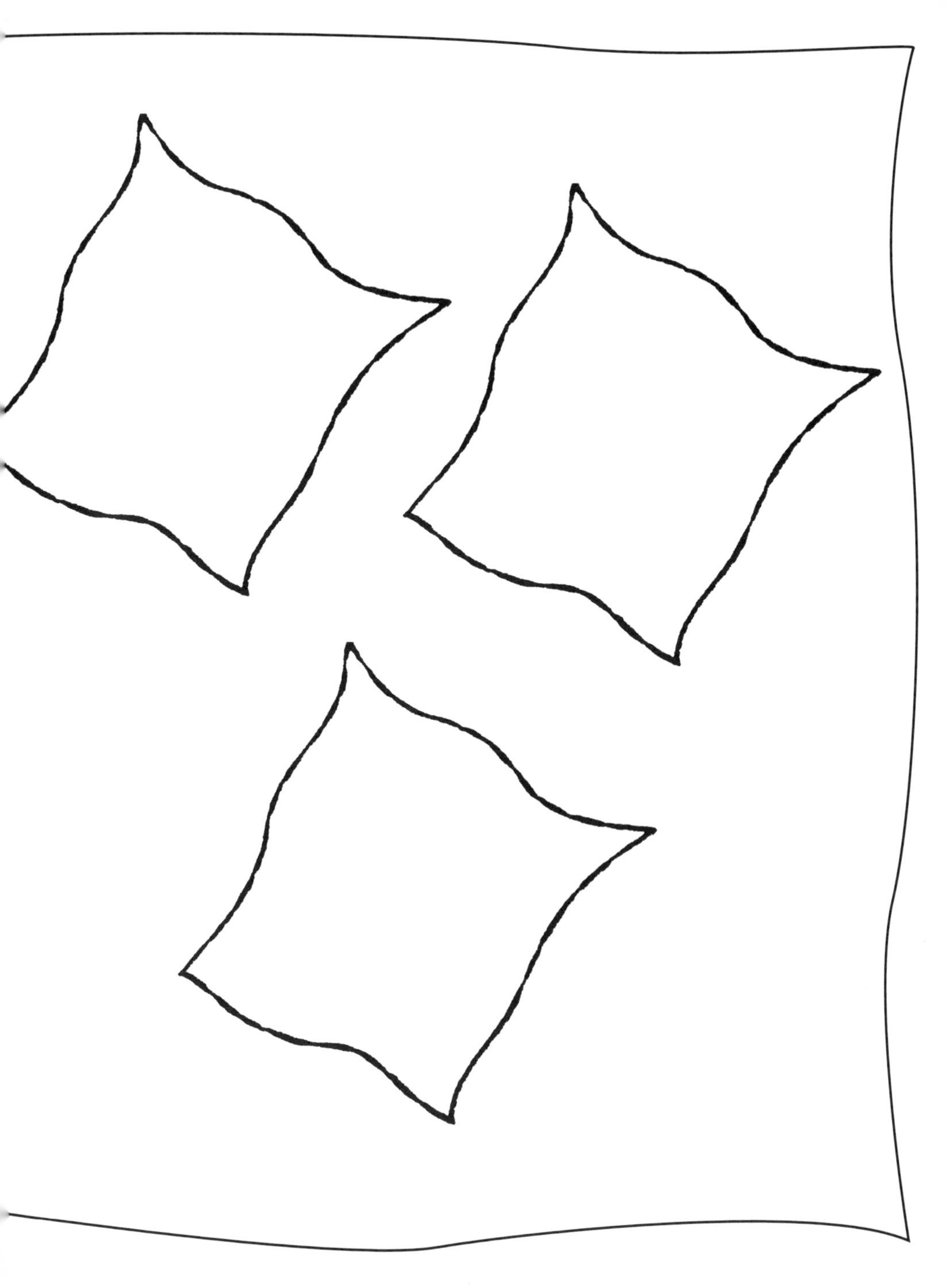

There are no ships to plunder at the moment so pirates on this ship have taken up knitting. Draw what they made.

Draw a pirate swabbing the deck.

Draw some cake decorations
for a pirate's birthday cake.

Draw a pirate's poem.

Draw a pirate or two in this giant fish's tummy.

Draw a message in this bottle.

There are mysterious footprints on this desert island. Draw their owner.

Grace O'Malley was a fierce Pirate Queen who patrolled the West of Ireland in the sixteenth century.

Draw who's hiding in this palm tree.

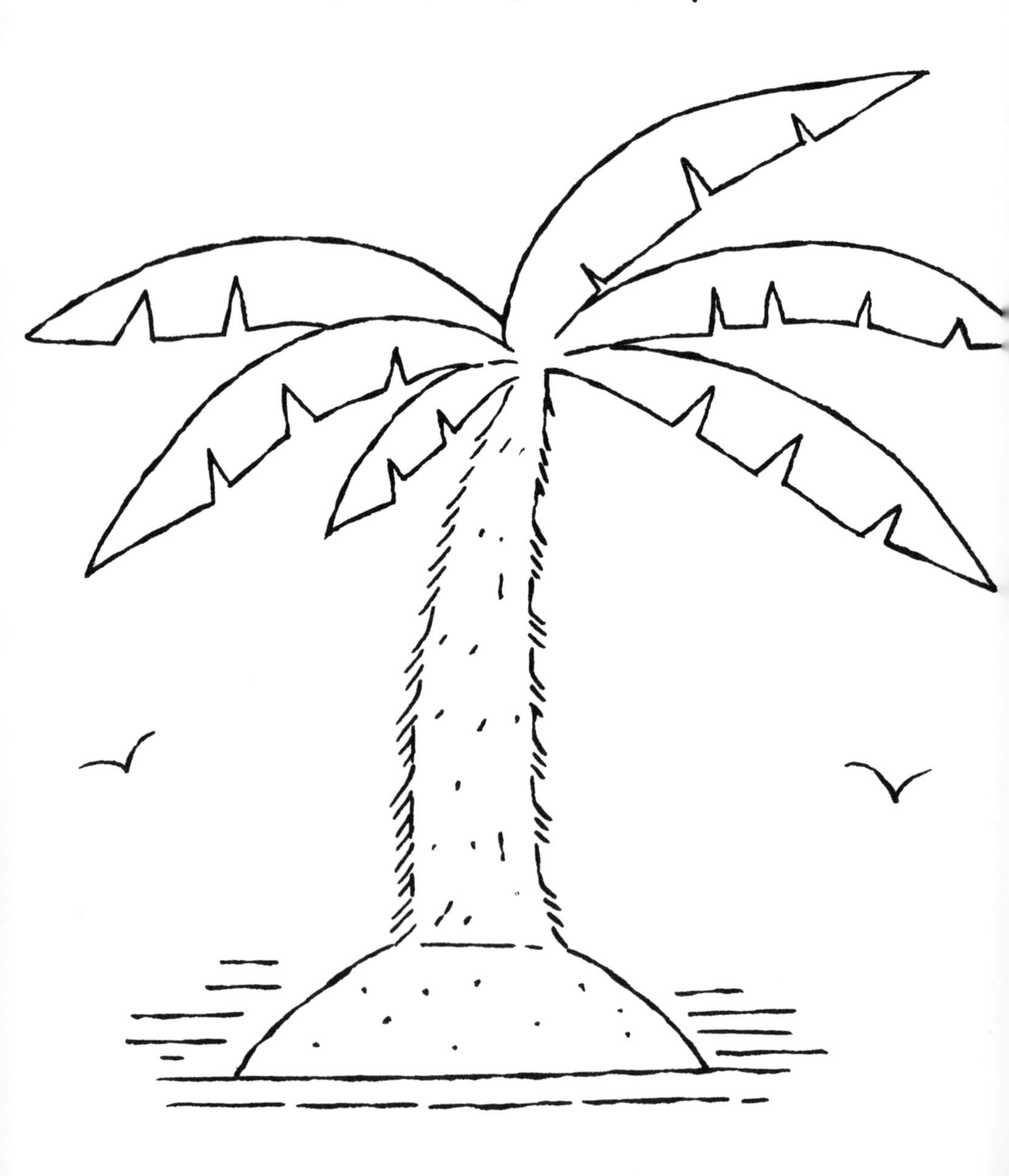

Draw a stowaway below
deck on the Nasty Nigel.

Draw some fish
in this lagoon.

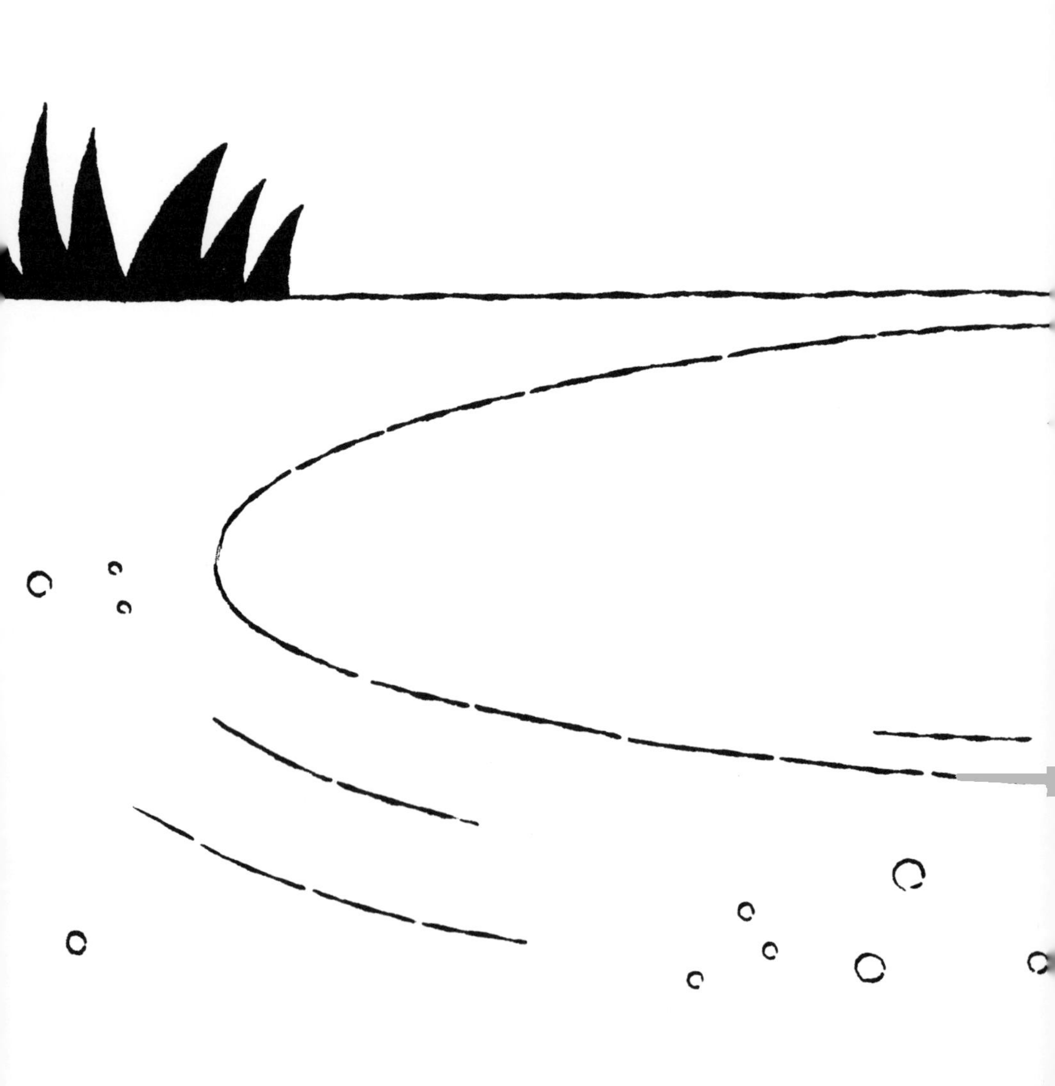

Draw some stars to steer your ship by.

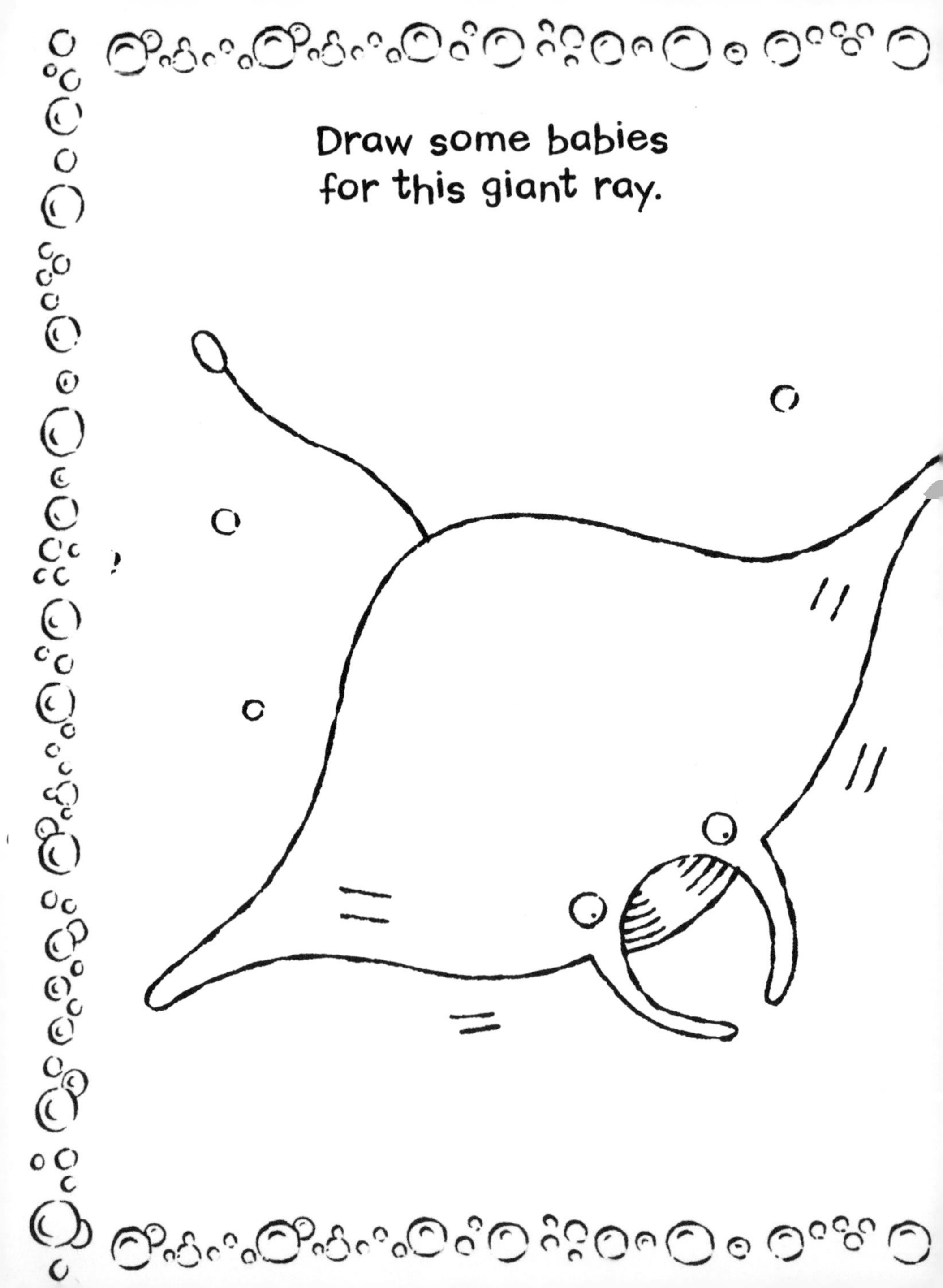
Draw some babies
for this giant ray.

Draw a pirate's sneeze.

YUCK!

Draw some young pirates on this seesaw in the pirates' playground.

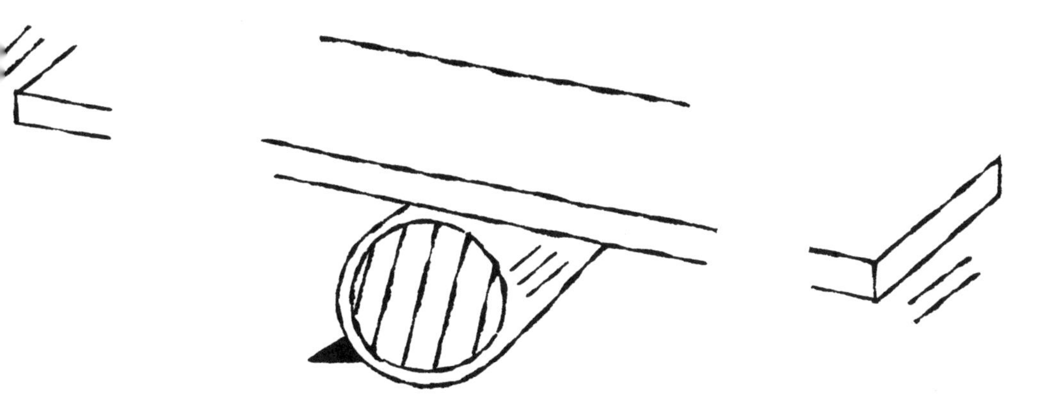

Draw a pirate having a bath – it didn't happen that often by the way!

Alfhild was a Viking pirate princess famous for being horribly fierce AND beautiful. Draw her!

Draw what's in these pirate jars.

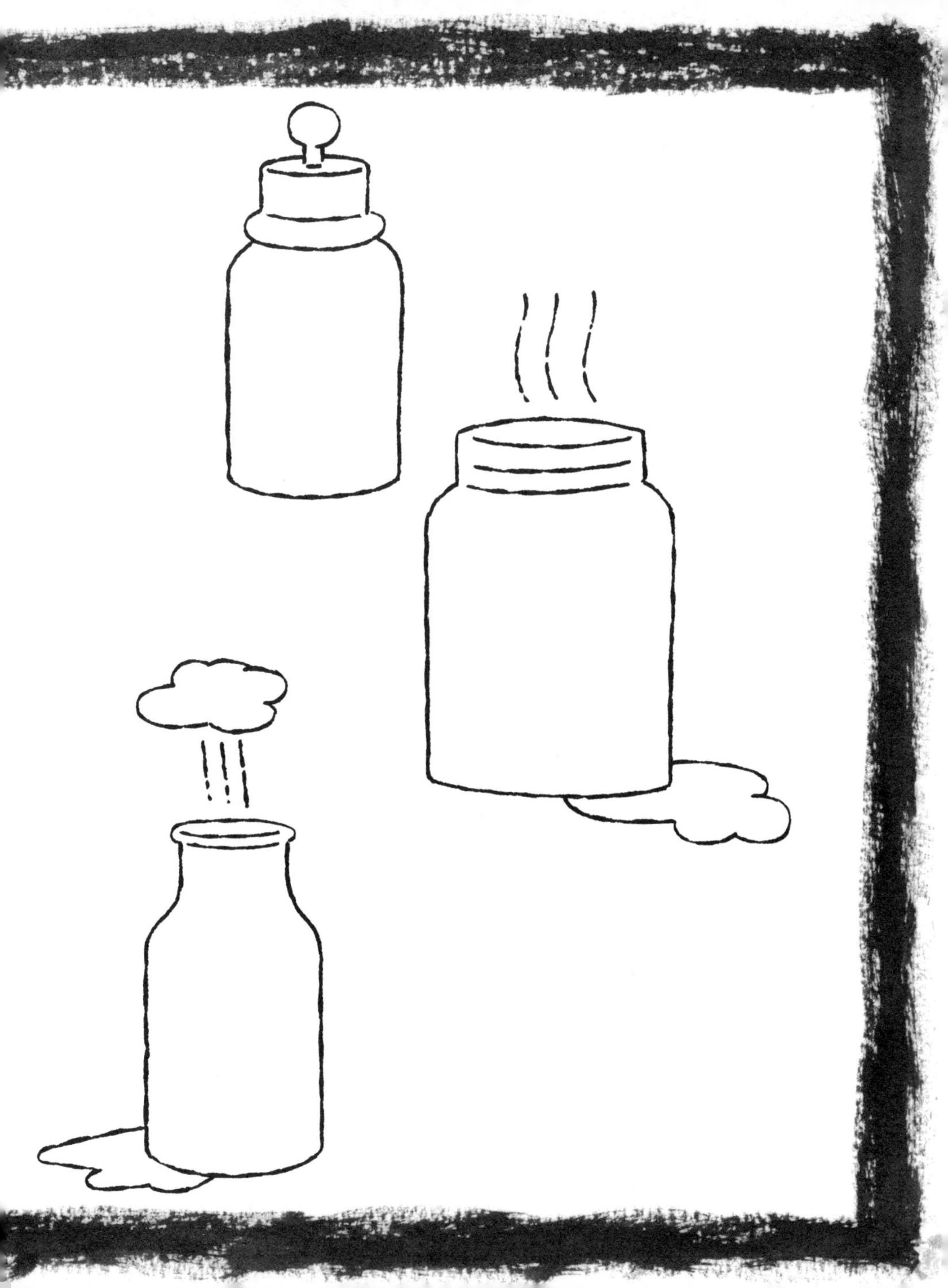

Draw a pirate Santa.

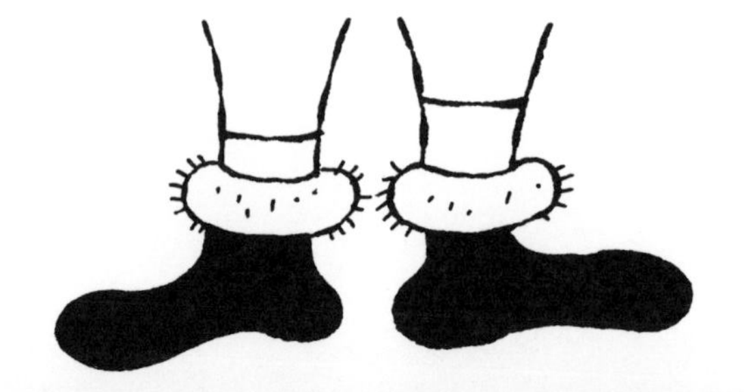

Draw some swashbuckling.

When pirate Henry Morgan and his crew were stranded without food, they stewed and ate their leather satchels.

Draw a pirate doing a handstand.

Draw a ship's cat
and give it a name.

Capt'n Dirty Dierdre is determined her crew will win the Bushiest Beard and Twirliest Moustache Competition this year. Draw some stylish suggestions for them.

Twentieth century Chinese pirate Lai Choi San appeared as the character "Dragon Lady" in an American comic strip.

I'm in training.

Draw a ship in this bottle.

When pirates went ashore they liked to have a glass (or six) of grog at the Maggoty Biscuit Inn. Draw a sign to hang outside the inn.

Draw some pirate treasure discovered in this pit.

These knots have different names. Draw some knots of your own and name them!

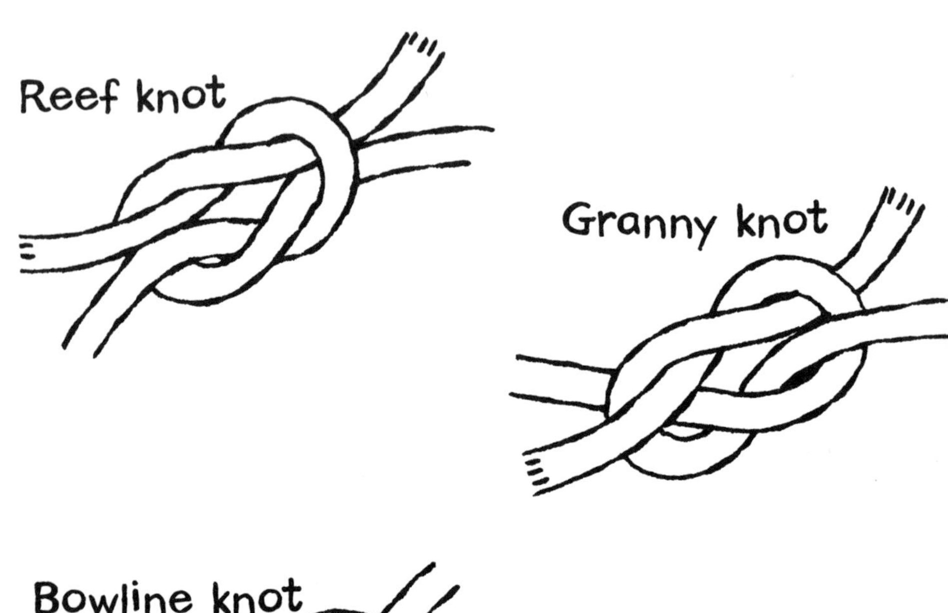

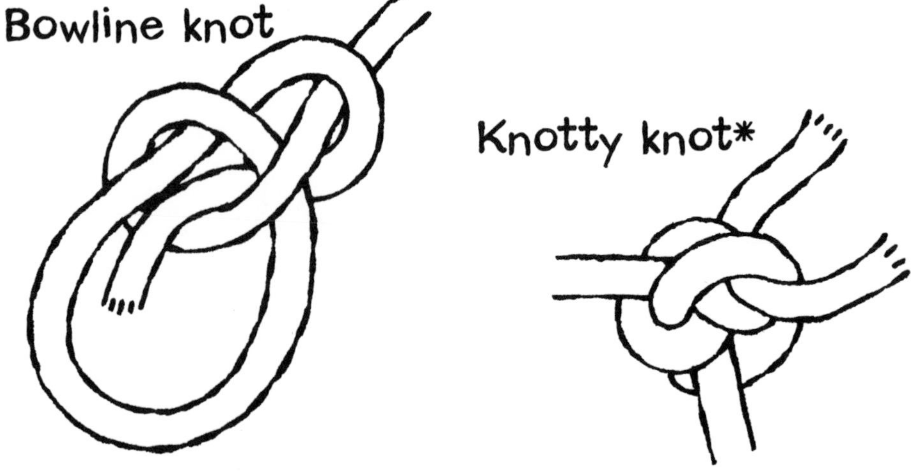

* OK, I made that one up.

Draw some pirates at a Rusty Cutlass drawing workshop.

A popular pirate drink was bomboo, made of rum, sugar and nutmeg.

Uh oh! Some of the old pirates are making trouble at the Pirates Retirement Home. Draw them!

Out of my way, ye swabs!

Draw a cover for a book of pirate's memoirs.

Make up some names for these ships.

Draw what a
pirate smells like.

Draw some other stinky
things onboard.

Draw your crew.

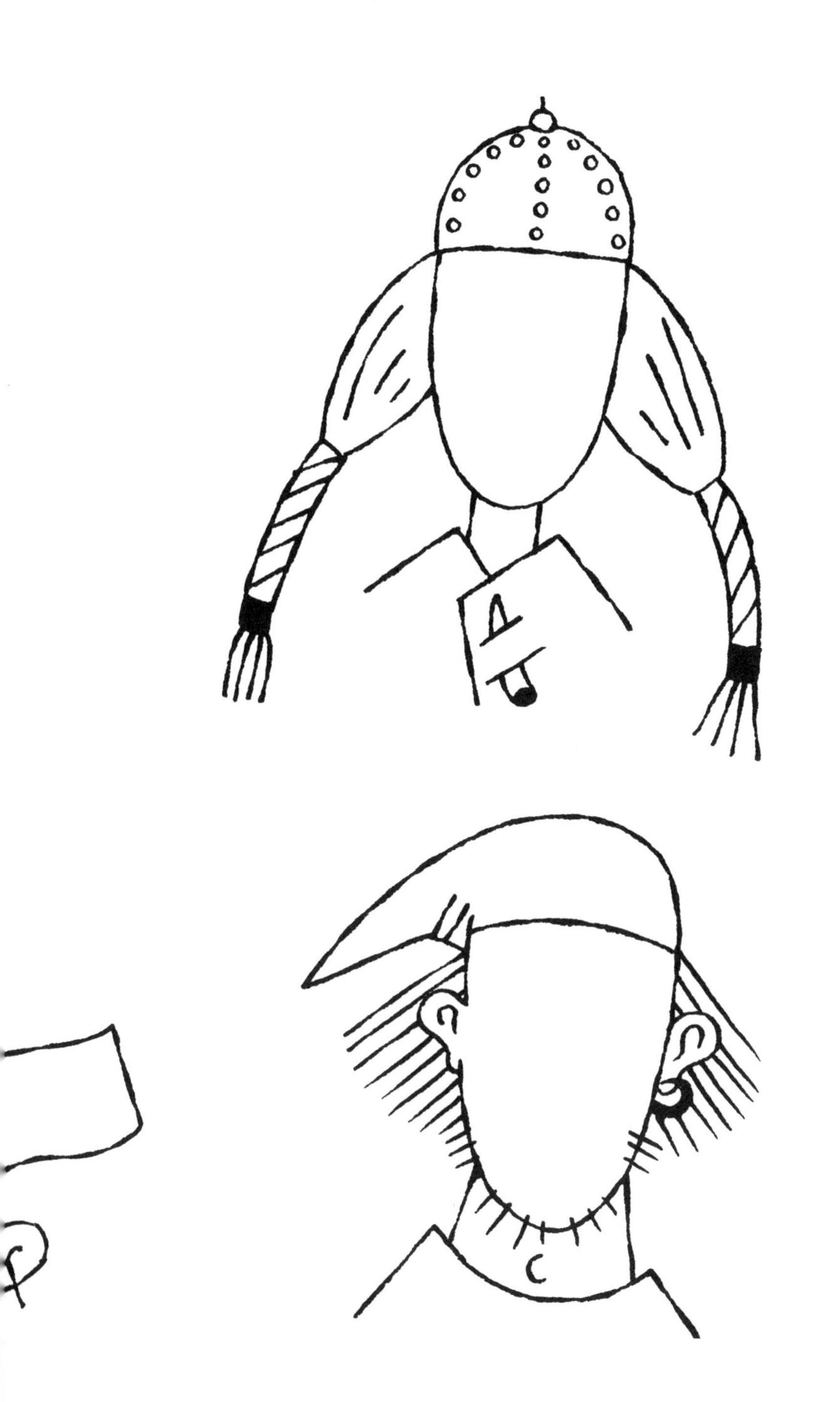

Wait! A latecomer has won the tug o' war competition.

Ooh!

I love it when pirates fall overboard. Yum Yum!